THE EMPEROR'S
NEW CLOTHES

Adapted from Hans Christian Andersen
and illustrated by

JANET STEVENS

HOLIDAY HOUSE/NEW YORK

For Margery
and Holiday House

Library of Congress Cataloging in Publication Data

Stevens, Janet.
    The emperor's new clothes.

    Summary: Two rascals sell a vain emperor an invisible
suit of clothes.
    1. Children's stories, Danish.   [1. Fairy tales]
I. Andersen, H. C. (Hans Christian), 1805-1875.   Kejserens
nye klae der.   II. Title.
PZ8.S614Em   1985   [E]   85-728
ISBN 0-8234-0566-4

Many, many years ago there lived an emperor who spent all of his time and all of his money on clothes.

Instead of taking care of his kingdom, he stood in front of his mirror admiring himself. He owned a different outfit for every hour of the day.

One morning, two foxes dressed as weavers came to visit the emperor. They were scoundrels who wanted to cheat him out of some of his wealth.

"We have heard that you love clothes," they said. "For the right price, we can weave you some beautiful magic cloth."

The emperor's small eyes gleamed. "Magic cloth?" he said. "I've never heard of that. Tell me more."

The weavers leaned closer and whispered, "This magic cloth can help you find out who's worthy and unworthy in your kingdom. Those who can see the cloth are smart and good at what they do. Those who can't see it are stupid and should be fired."

The emperor rubbed his chin and straightened his wig.

"There probably are some stupid people in my kingdom I should fire," he mused. "Could you make me a new outfit from your magic cloth?"

"Yes!" said the two foxes, licking their chops. "But, before we begin to weave, you must pay us a large sum. We also need the finest silk and gold threads that money can buy."

"Take this bag of gold," said the emperor, "and I'll order the thread immediately." He wiggled his ears and clicked his hooves at the thought of having a new expensive suit.

When the thread arrived, the two foxes stashed it in their knapsacks instead of putting it on the looms. Then they sat down and pretended to weave the magic cloth. The scoundrels looked like they were busy, but they were really weaving nothing at all. Their looms were empty.

Day after day, as the foxes pretended to weave, news of the magic cloth traveled through the kingdom. The villagers were curious to see the emperor's new clothes. They were anxious to find out if they were stupid or not, and whether they would lose their jobs.

One morning, the emperor woke up and wondered, "How is my cloth coming along? I think I'll go visit the weavers." But when he remembered what they'd told him, his lips twitched and his tail curled. "What if I can't see the cloth?" he thought. "That would mean I am stupid and I'd have to fire myself. I'd better send the prime minister instead."

After breakfast, the prime minister went to visit the weavers.
As usual, they were busy weaving nothing on their empty looms,
but the poor prime minister didn't know that. He closed his eyes
and opened them wide.

"Bless my hump, I don't see a thing," he thought.

The scoundrels pointed to the empty looms and said, "Come
closer and admire the brilliant colors and the splendid patterns."

The prime minister took off his glasses and wiped them with his handkerchief. Then he put them back on and looked again, but still he could see nothing.

"Oh, dear," he muttered to himself. "I thought I was doing a good job as prime minister, and no one's ever called me stupid. But I guess I'm a failure. I'd better not tell anyone I can't see the cloth. Otherwise, I'll get fired."

"What do you think of it?" asked the scoundrels. "Do you think it's fit for an emperor?"

"Y-y-yes," stammered the prime minister. "It's b-b-beautiful. The most b-b-beautiful cloth I've ever seen. I'll g-g-go tell the emperor at once."

"Please tell him also that we need more silk and gold threads," said the weavers.

"Right away," said the prime minister, shuffling out of the room as fast as he could.

The emperor clapped like a child when the prime minister told him about the beautiful magic cloth. He sent the weavers more thread.

Again, the two scoundrels stuffed it into their knapsacks instead of using it on the looms.

In a few days, the emperor ordered his councillor to find out when the cloth would be ready.

The councillor squinted at the empty looms. No matter how hard he strained to see the cloth, he couldn't see a thing. But the poor councillor didn't know he was being tricked.

"Isn't this cloth extraordinary?" asked the weavers.

Like the prime minister, the councillor worried that since he couldn't see what was on the looms, he was either very stupid or might lose his job. He too decided to pretend he had seen the cloth.

"Well, what do you think of it?" asked the weavers.

The councillor fidgeted with his mustache. "Why, it's, it's . . . *magnifique*," he said. He flubbered and blubbered out of the room and hurried to tell the emperor about the magic cloth.

Finally, the emperor couldn't wait any longer. He gathered together the prime minister, the councillor, and the rest of the court. They paraded to the great room where the weavers were working.

When the two foxes saw them coming, their fingers flew over the empty looms, pretending to finish the cloth.

"You came at just the right moment," they said to the emperor. "We are done."

The prime minister stepped forward and pointed. "Notice the
brilliant colors, your majesty," he said.

"And the splendid patterns," added the councillor.

The emperor gulped. He couldn't see a thing. His skin grew
pinker. His tail curled and uncurled.

"Oh, no," he squealed to himself. "This is a royal disaster. Am
I unfit to be emperor? This will never do. I mustn't tell anyone I
can't see a thing."

So out loud he said, "The cloth is exquisite. You must make my new clothes immediately. I need them for the great procession that takes place next Saturday."

Like the emperor, the court stared at the looms, but they couldn't see anything either. They too said, "It's exquisite," because nobody wanted to look stupid or be fired. The emperor pretended to share in the crowd's happiness and named the two weavers royal knights of the loom.

The night before the procession, the scoundrels stayed up all night, pretending to work. They lit the room with candles so everyone could see how busy they were. They pretended to roll the cloth off the looms. They cut the air with their big scissors, and sewed with needles that had no thread. Finally, they were finished.

The emperor and his court came to see the new clothes.

The scoundrels lifted their arms, pretending to hold up a pair of new pants, a new robe, and a new train.

"Here's your beautiful outfit," they said to the emperor. "It is as light as cobwebs. It will feel as if you are wearing nothing at all, but that's the wonderful thing about clothes sewn from magic cloth."

"Yes, indeed," agreed the court, but they saw nothing, for there was nothing to see.

"Would you let us remove your clothes, your majesty," asked the weavers, "so you can try on your new outfit?"

The emperor did as he was asked, and the weavers pretended to dress him. The emperor stood in front of the mirror, admiring the new clothes he couldn't see.

"How pink and perfect you look!" cried the prime minister.

"It fits like a second skin," added the councillor.

Though they could see nothing, everybody agreed that the emperor had never looked better.

As the procession began, the two royal attendants pretended to pick up the invisible train. The emperor marched through the streets under his royal red canopy. At first the villagers were silent. Nobody was willing to admit they couldn't see anything on the emperor. But finally they cried, "What beautiful new clothes. How magnificent. How well they fit."

Then a little bear shouted, "But he doesn't have anything on!"

Silence swept through the crowd.

"My little bear speaks the truth," said the father bear.

The people started to whisper, "The emperor doesn't have anything on."

Word spread rapidly, and soon the crowd was buzzing with the news: "The emperor doesn't have anything on!"

Then, together, everyone cried, "HE HAS NOTHING ON AT ALL!"

The emperor blushed until he was almost as red as the canopy above him. He realized that what the crowd said was true, and that he had been tricked by the two weavers. He wanted to run away, but he knew he must stay and do his job, since he *was* the emperor. He pulled in his stomach, and held his head high as he continued to lead the procession. The royal attendants followed, still holding the train that wasn't there.